TODAY IN SPOOKY HALLOWEEN HISTORY

WRITTEN BY

ROB "ROBBY ACES" ACEVEDO

WITH ART BY

G. SPOSTO

OCTOBER

1st

ON THIS DAY IN 1991,
JEFFREY DAHMER,
POSSESSED BY A DARK AND POWERFUL URGE...
SNAPPED INTO A
SLIM JIM.
oOoo-EEEE-oOoo... SPOOKY!!

OCTOBER

2ND

ON THIS DAY IN 1967,
IN POINT PLEASANT, VIRGINIA,
THE MOTHMAN
WAS SPOTTED FEASTING ON
THE REMAINS OF AN UNWITTING
ARGYLE SWEATER!

oOoo·EEEE·oOoo...SPOOKY!!

OCTOBER

3RD

ON THIS DAY IN 1869,
VOODOO QUEEN
MARIE LAVEAU
TURNED A FROG INTO A GENTLEMAN...
BY AFFIXING A DAINTY TOP HAT TO ITS HEAD!
oOoo-EEEE-oOoo... SPOOKY!!

OCTOBER

4TH

ON THIS DAY IN 1818,
MAD DOCTOR
VICTOR FRANKENSTEIN,
USING THE TERRIFYING POWER OF
LIGHTNING AND DISCARDED SLABS...
...OF CHEESE... CREATED A
GRILLED CHEESE SANDWICH.
IT WAS A MONSTER.
OFF
oOoo-EEEE-oOoo... SPOOKY!!

OCTOBER
5TH

ON THIS DAY IN 1977,
IN AMITYVILLE, NY, A HORRIFIED FAMILY
PILED INTO THEIR MINIVAN IN THE
MIDDLE OF TORRENTIAL RAINS
AND DROVE OUT OF TOWN, NEVER TO RETURN...
WHEN THE ALL-YOU-CAN-EAT BUFFET AT
THE LOCAL BENIHANA RAN OUT OF FOOD!
BENIHANA
oOoo-EEEE-oOoo... SPOOKY!!

OCTOBER

6TH

ON THIS DAY IN 1956,
IN CHICAGO, A NERVOUS YOUNG BOY NAMED
STEPHEN KING
SOILED HIMSELF DURING A LIVE TAPING
OF THE BOZO SHOW.
"**IT," HE CRIED!
**IT!!
oOoo-EEEE-oOoo... SPooKY!!

OCTOBER

7TH

ON THIS DAY IN 1967,
HORROR MOVIE DIRECTOR
GEORGE ROMERO,
WHILE EMPLOYED AT A HOCKEY RINK,
WAS SLOWLY, AND TERRIFYINGLY CHASED
ACROSS THE ICE BY AN UNMANNED
ZAMBONI... A TRUE ZOMBONI!

oOoo-EEEE-oOoo... SPOOKY!!

OCTOBER

8th

ON THIS DAY IN 1971,
LINUS SACRIFICED HIS BLANKET
IN A DESPERATE ATTEMPT TO
SUMMON THE
GREAT PUMPKIN.
AND SHORTLY BEFORE MIDNIGHT,
UNBIDDEN, SALLY BROUGHT HIM AN ENTEMANN'S
PUMPKIN LOAF.
oOoo-EEEE-oOoo... SPOOKY!!

OCTOBER 9TH

ON THIS DAY IN 1591,
THE COLONY OF SKYNARD, ALABAMA
DISAPPEARED.
THE ONLY TRACE OF ITS INHABITANTS
WAS A STONE UPON WHICH WAS SCRAWLED THE
STRANGE AND CRYPTIC WORD
"FREEBIRD."
FREEBIRD
oOoo-EEEE-oOoo... SPOOKY!!

OCTOBER

10TH

ON THIS DAY IN 740 C.E.,
AL RAZED "THE MAD ARAB",
AUTHOR OF
THE NECRONOMICON
RECEIVED A HARROWING VISION OF THE FUTURE.
1272 YEARS LATER, ARAB RELIGIOUS SCHOLARS REALIZED
THE CRYPTIC VISION WAS A SCENE-FOR-SCENE
RETELLING OF THE FIRST EPISODE OF
EVERYBODY LOVES RAYMOND.
oOoo-EEEE-oOoo... SPOOKY!!

OCTOBER
11TH

ON THIS DAY IN 1909,
IN TRENTON, THE JERSEY DEVIL
WAS SPOTTED SINGING "SWING LOW,
SWEET CHARIOT" AND DRESSED
TO THE NINES!
Jazz
AND WHAT DID I SEE?
I LOOKED OVER JORDAN
COMIN' FOR TO CARRY ME
HOOO OOOO OME?
oOoo-EEEE-oOoo... Spooky!!

OCTOBER

12TH

ON THIS DAY IN 1983,
RICHARD "THE NIGHT STALKER" RAMIREZ
STALKED
THE STREETS OF LOS ANGELES...
IN SEARCH OF A FRAGGLE ROCK LUNCH BOX!
HOW MUCH?
FRAGGLE ROCK
6.66
oOoo-EEEE-oOoo... SPOOKY!!

OCTOBER

13th

ON THIS DAY IN 1997, THE CHUBACABRA WENT VEGAN.
I'M NEVER GIVING UP MEAT.
UGH.
oOoo-EEEE-oOoo... SPooky!!

OCTOBER

14TH

ON THIS DAY IN 2004,
IN SCOTLAND, FROM DEEP BELOW
THE DEPTHS OF LOCH NESS,
AS DOZENS OF SIGHTSEERS LOOKED ON,
A MONSTER... ENERGY DRINK
ROSE TO THE SURFACE.

oOoo-EEEE-oOoo... SPOOKY!!

OCTOBER
15TH

ON THIS DAY IN 1773, THE HELLFIRE CLUB HELD A PICNIC WITH A SCARY NEW DESSERT...
ICED CREAM.
oOoo-EEEE-oOoo... SPOOKY!!

OCTOBER 16TH

ON THIS DAY IN 1901,
H.P. LOVECRAFT'S DOG
HAD A PUPPY.
HE NAMED IT
CTHULHU.

oOoo-EEEE-oOoo... SpooKy!!

OCTOBER 17TH

ON THIS DAY IN 1986,
REVEREND JERRY FALWELL
DISCOVERED THAT, WHEN PLAYED BACKWARDS,
OZZY OSBOURNE'S "BARK AT THE MOON"
CONTAINED A HIDDEN MESSAGE
REVEALING THE RECIPE FOR
FRANKENBERRY
CEREAL.
1 PART FLOUR TO 6 PARTS SUGAR...
3 ML RED DYE NO. 2...
oOoo-EEEE-oOoo... SPOOKY!!

OCTOBER

18th

ON THIS DAY IN 1925,
BLACK MAGICIAN
ALEISTER CROWLEY
SUMMONED... A MAID...
TO DARN HIS SOCKS.

oOoo-EEEE-oOoo... Spooky!!

OCTOBER

19th

ON THIS DAY IN 1582,
THE DIABOLICAL
DR. FAUSTUS
MADE A PACT WITH A DEVIL...ED EGG
WHILE DRUNK ON
GERMAN BEER!
MOM
oOoo-EEEE-oOoo... SPOOKY!!

OCTOBER 20TH

ON THIS DAY IN 1942,
ANTON LAVEY,
FOUNDER OF THE
CHURCH OF SATAN,
LEARNED TO RIDE A UNICYCLE!

oOoo-EEEE-oOoo... SPOOKY!!

OCTOBER
21ST

ON THIS DAY IN 1982,
AT A GATHERING OF ITALIAN WARLOCKS
LEGENDARY BLACK SABBATH SINGER
RONNIE JAMES DIO
SANG THE "MY LITTLE PONY"
THEME SONG.
oOoo-EEEE-oOoo... SPOOKY!!

OCTOBER

22ND

ON THIS DAY IN 1931,
FUTURE DELTA BLUES LEGEND
ROBERT JOHNSON
FINISHED A CROSSWORD PUZZLE
AT THE CROSSROADS AT MIDNIGHT
WITH THE 6-LETTER WORD FOR A
MUSICAL INSTRUMENT.

oOoo-EEEE-oOoo... SPOOKY!!

OCTOBER

23RD

ON THIS DAY IN 1730,
IN SLEEPY HOLLOW, ICHABOD CRANE
WENT TO BED EARLY... AND THE
HEADLESS HORSEMAN
MOPED ABOUT THE TOWN BRIDGE UNTIL
SUNRISE, SIGHING LONGINGLY.
oOoo-EEEE-oOoo... SPOOKY!!

OCTOBER
24TH

ON THIS DAY IN 1959,
BELA LEGOSI AND BORIS KARLOFF
PLAYED BACKGAMMON.
LEGOSI WON.
KARLOFF CRIED.

oOoo-EEEE-oOoo... SPOOKY!!

OCTOBER

25TH

ON THIS DAY IN 1961, SPOOKY SINGER "SCREAMIN'" JAY HAWKINS WHISPERED:
WHY, DOESN'T LITTLE RICHARD INVITE ME OVER ANYMORE?
AM I TOO LOUD?
oOoo-EEEE-oOoo... SPOOKY!!

OCTOBER
26TH

ON THIS DAY IN 1898,
HOPING TO CAPITALIZE ON THE
WANING DECADE'S SPIRITUALISM
AND WINDOW-CLEANING CRAZES,
PARKER BROTHERS PATENTED THE
"SQUEEGEE BOARD"
...FUN FOR AGES 6 TO 60.

oOoo-EEEE-oOoo... SPOOKY!!

OCTOBER

27TH

ON THIS DAY IN 1872,
WRITER EDGAR ALLAN POE,
AS A RAVEN WATCHED ON,
ATE A HAM SANDWICH.
ALONE.
oOoo-EEEE-oOoo... SPOOKY!!

OCTOBER

28TH

ON THIS DAY IN 1977,
SPOOKY PERFORMANCE ARTIST
AND 33RD DEGREE MASON
GALLAGHER
BRUTALLY SMASHED A WATERMELON
IN FRONT OF 100S OF
HORRIFIED ONLOOKERS.
THUS BEGAN A REIGN OF TERROR...
oOoo-EEEE-oOoo... SPOOKY!!

OCTOBER 29TH

ON THIS DAY IN 1983,
ON THE SET OF
"THRILLER,"
SPOOKY ACTOR VINCENT PRICE,
WITH A CRAZED LOOK IN HIS EYE,
REFUSED MICHAEL JACKSON'S OFFER
OF A PEPSI, WHISPERING,
" THE HOUNDS OF HELL PREFER
COCA COLA."
oOoo - EEEE - oOoo... SpooKy!!

October 30th

ON THIS DAY IN 1981,
JASON VOORHES
TOOK AN AXE AT CAMP CRYSTAL LAKE
AND VIOLENTLY BLUDGEONED SOME LOGS
AFTER FAILING TO SUCCESSFULLY
PITCH
A
TENT!
oOoo-EEEE-oOoo... SPOOKY!!

OCTOBER
31ST

ON THIS DAY IN 2012,
SPOOKY RADIO HOST
DR. DEMENTO
WENT
SANE.
WHAT AM I DOING WITH MY LIFE?
oOoo-EEEE-oOoo... SPOOKY!!

ROBERT "ROBBY ACES" ALSTRUM-ACEVEDO

IS A WRITER AND COMEDIAN
CURRENTLY LIVING IN LAS VEGAS, NEVADA.

HE HAS PERFORMED COMEDY
IN TOKYO, DUBLIN, NEW YORK,
AND ON THE ROAD THROUGHOUT THE U.S.

HE CAN BE FOUND ON THE WEB AT VANILLATINO.COM
OR ON INSTAGRAM - @ROBBYACES_STANDUP

GINA SPOSTO

IS A DESIGNER, MULTIMEDIA VISUAL
ARTIST, AND ILLUSTRATOR
BASED IN LOS ANGELES, CALIFORNIA.

SHE HAS TWO INSTAGRAM ACCOUNTS:

@GREATGRANDADDYG FOR FINE ART AND DESIGN,
&
@POISONED.ART.FROG FOR CARTOONS